MW01077854

ST.IS

The First Book

LISA SAMSON

LEN SWEET

The Salish Sea Press

Words of Good Will

St.Is tells the story of Jesus' birth from the unique perspective of Issy, Mary's delightful and loyal donkey. Told with delight and whimsy, *St.Is* is Biblical truth wrapped in narrative brilliance. The first of a series of books, *St.Is* will stir your imagination and whet your appetite for more.

~Bryce Ashlin-Mayo, Lead Pastor of Westlife Church and author of *Digital Mission: A Practical Guide for Ministry Online*. bryceashlinmayo.com

Lisa Samson and Leonard Sweet tell an old, old story in a new way. Readers of *St.Is*, hear the aged and familiar story of Jesus' birth. But this time, it is heard through the voice of the donkey that carried Mary to Bethlehem. With wit and wisdom—and a good dose of healthy ingenuity—Samson and Sweet open the eyes, ears, and hearts of the reader to a story that has too often become stilted and stale. This book not only teaches, it also tickles the imagination and throws open the windows, allowing The Breath of fresh air to bring a cleansing breeze to dust off the story we know so well.

~Dr. Dyton L. Owen, Pastor, Author

While it might initially seem profane to tell the story of Jesus from the perspective of an ass, this engaging tale manages to be reverently faithful to the old, old story while expounding on it with a dynamic approach that draws us to consider, indeed to savor, nuances of depth we have not reached before. This is a rich narrative that I anticipate pondering and rereading many times, and sharing aloud with my grandson. It is story elevated to the level of conceptual art, testament to the living and active Word of God. I look forward to hearing more from Is.

~Beth McKinnon, Grandmother and Hospice Nurse.

Just finished reading *St.Is*. This will make great reading for all seven of my grandkids, from age 6 to 15. My mother and dad will also enjoy it. My Christmas shopping is complete.

~Mike Krost

The cover says it all! I guarantee you will smile, feel joy and be blessed with gratitude after reading about Issy (or Is) the donkey and Mary the mother of Jesus. We are asked to imagine the story of the birth of Jesus through the eyes of a donkey. Mary loves Issy, Issy loves Mary and they both love Jesus. That love is the thread of truth that weaves through page after page. This book is a delight to the eyes and gladness for the heart. Thank you Lisa and Len!

~ Chris Miller, grandparent, retired, but retreaded as a Minister of Pastoral Care

Thank you so much for sharing this precious story! I love the simplicity intertwined with the depth and the creativity of the nonlinear narrative. The little nuggets of "jenny wisdom" are priceless but the absolute best part? The ending! So good.

~ Jen McNab, Co-Creator, Toward Thriving, LLC

Captivating! I read until my eyes couldn't take anymore then finished the book this morning. It is hard to find the best words without sounding trite. I love dear *St.Is* and her bright insight. I cannot wait to order multiple copies to both put on my shelf and give to others to offer hope in this dark time of great opportunity! AMAZING artwork! Simple, clear, powerful, Divine! Blessings all!

~ Donna Lynne Vaux, LLP Retired and now free to dabble in expressions of faith through words, paints, and photos.

What a fun and unique look at the timeless story of Christmas. Great use of imagination firmly rooted in the truth of God's word. I loved it.

~ Shaun Hart, Pastor, Hockinson Community Church

I so enjoyed reading the story of *St.Is*. It's a wonderful story of an ancient Donkey who has such spiritual insight into so many heavenly hosts around her throughout her many adventures. Mary's unconditional love is a true blessing in her old age. I can't wait to read the next 'chapter/book' for Easter.

~ Mary Ann Miller, Kitchener, ON, Canada

St.Is

ISBN: 978-1-63613-000-2

Copyright © 2020 by Lisa Samson and Leonard Sweet. All rights reserved.

First published in the United States November, 2020, by The Salish Sea Press, a division of SpiritVenture Ministries, Box 1493, Absecon, NJ 08201.

Acknowledgment

We are especially grateful for and to
Dr. Myrtle Merritt
who believed in this project from the start.

Acknowledgment

We are especially grateful for and to
Dr. Myrtle Merritt
who believed in this project from the start.

Dedication

To the big bosses:

Zeus, Thor, Hanna, and Hiro.

Here We Go!

Once upon a journey to the King of Moab, the prophet Balaam beat his donkey. Now when one reads his story in the scriptures of the Hebrew people, the story is more about Balaam than the donkey, a she-donkey. Yet, who became the famous one? The creature who came to be known as Balaam's Ass. Why?

Because she did something nobody allows for even to this day, except in fairy tales when the clock strikes midnight.

This sweet donkey, born ten years earlier, bedded down nightly in the stable of a family with three active children, a bouncy-bodied mother, a father with a magnificent laugh, and a toothless old woman that claimed to be a long-lost great-aunt. Everyone doubted that, but nobody had the heart to really find out for sure if she was telling the truth—for then as now, loving souls become family quickly enough. And this great-aunt fed the donkey, patted her, and sang songs as she did so.

The donkey was, nevertheless, the beast of burden. When the family needed her because their load was too heavy to carry, the donkey carried it for them, and she took her turn at the village grain mill. Faithful and bright, she had given the family donkeys to raise and sell over the years, and they loved her, for this was a *special donkey* they said to others. Not that anybody else could see it. They all loved one another, and that was what mattered.

One day, misfortune interrupted the family's good fortune and the land's bounty. The donkey was bedding down for the night in the stable when terrible words, formed in the mouth of the father, came forth.

"Starlight," for that was her name, "either needs to be sold or eaten. We can barely feed ourselves any longer."

The old woman rushed to the donkey's side (for stables were just another room of the house back then, gated to keep the animals in but open to allow for heat when the nights grew cold).

The oldest daughter wept, the youngest boy kicked his father in the shin, the middle girl started yelling. The donkey might have yelled, too, except at that time, she existed in the manner of most other donkeys in her world, only worried about good feed, fresh water, and rest. And like the other donkeys in the world, she was aware of danger. She tuned into their tone of voice.

"I don't think anybody will be able to swallow a bite," the mother said. "We love Starlight. Let's calm down."

Everyone agreed and all three children, the father, and the beloved old aunt settled down.

The donkey laid her head back on the straw.

Thankfully for the donkey, and sadly for all, rather than eat her, the family sold her to a man named Balaam.

She carried him on her back for many years. An important man, Balaam "divined" the will of God for a fee. He also spoke the will of God for free to officials of all types by hearing within himself the voice of God. This was as unenjoyable as one might suspect, for speaking something untrue in the name of God would dry up his tongue like a vine no longer watered from the heavens. That's the last thing a prophet-for-hire wants.

Called by the King of Moab to curse the tribes of Israel who had gathered at the mouth of the land of Canaan after walking around the wilderness for forty years, Balaam was promised a handsome reward. God wasn't inclined to cooperate and said a perfect, *no*. But Balaam, blinded by the riches he might have received, put fresh words in God's mouth concerning his own mission. He believed The Most High decided otherwise than had been spoken, so he traveled to Moab to utter the words of the Lord.

But God doesn't change his mind. Even the donkey, who was only called Donkey at this point, knew as much. Still, she had no choice but to bear him toward the summoning King.

Balaam and the donkey traveled upon a narrow path through vineyards. The day was warm; the prophet ate dried dates from a sack.

The donkey slowed, then veered onto a smaller trail.

"What is this, Donkey?" Balaam cried.

She stopped and would have stayed there, except Balaam beat her with a stick hard enough she decided to take her chances back on the path. They traveled a little further between vineyard walls and the donkey stopped once more, pinning Balaam's foot to the wall.

What did I ever do to you?

"Again? What are you doing?" Balaam beat the donkey again.

The little donkey took a few steps, and froze. Unable to move sideways due to the closeness of the walls, and refusing to move forward, she folded her legs beneath her and lay her head on the trail.

A third time, Balaam beat her upon her thigh. "You horrible creature!" Over and over he slammed his stick. "I didn't—" *slam* "—need—" *crack* "—this—" *pop* "—today!"

The donkey turned her head and opened her mouth. A squeak emerged, but instead of the ensuing braying Balaam expected, words came forth. Human words.

"Why do you treat me so harshly when all I have done these years is serve you faithfully?"

The prophet froze. Cudgel high and ready to strike, he opened his mouth. He looked around to see if he was the only one who heard. Trying to convince himself he heard what he thought he had heard, the words, "If it wasn't for that donkey, you'd be dead, prophet!" surrounded him. The words pierced through him in sparks and points as an angel appeared in splendor and strength, sword outstretched!

This was not, by far, the prophet Balaam's best day.

"You have disobeyed God in listening to the King of Moab's summons. However, you may continue to Moab, but under no circumstances are you to speak anything to the King other than what God says."

The donkey arose and they moved forward with no more beatings, "If only to keep that talking from ever happening again," Balaam told her. "On hindsight, that was more upsetting than the angel."

Some people, thought the donkey, and surprised herself.

Balaam delivered his message. The King of Moab was not pleased to hear God wanted to bless the Israelites and wasn't planning on sending them away anytime soon. The King was so displeased he sent Balaam home without one coin.

"This whole thing ended up costing *me* money," he said to the donkey, who, now that she *could* speak, decided not to. "I told you so," might lead to another round with the stick, talking animal or not. She was smart enough to know that now.

The Israelites eventually took over the land and the donkey with it. One evening, the angel appeared to the donkey again, this time humming with the love of God for even a lowly beast. "Will you carry the Lord's Messiah someday, little friend? You have proven yourself worthy of such a task."

The donkey bowed her head and spoke the last word she would say until the Messiah had need of her. "Yes," she said.

"Until then, carry on faithfully." The angel touched her forehead with a fingertip. "The Most High will never abandon you." And the angel departed, leaving the donkey to walk the earth wherever humankind decided she would go.

The little donkey did her best. But as the years collected, she wondered—especially on days she was overworked, overloaded, and neglected—if the Messiah had come and gone without her, or if God had forgotten.

IS

The burdens we donkeys bear
are never our own. Humans are
much the same, they just
utterly enjoy resenting the fact.

ST.IS

~ 1 ~

According to my family, I am Issy. I think of myself as *Is*. By this time in my life I have been assigned too many names to remember them all. *Is* will do just fine.

Numbered among those beasts called forth to serve the vast imagination of humankind, I bear the burdens of those two-footed beings who create images for their own eyes, notes for their own ears, flavors for their own tongues, and sensations for their own skin. They create empty spaces in which to place themselves and their gods as if they don't really belong here, to this land, to this vast and magnificent world they wake up in every day and mostly ignore.

Humans are strange.

All that intelligence floating around in a sea of oblivion—would the beasts could be so lucky. Though blessed with seeing eyes, humans seem to have lost the importance of using them somewhere along the way. They tend, one should note, to see the absence of what they think *should* be there. Consequently, I am bound to these creatures who create such monumental business for themselves they indenture the animal kingdom to carry it out. What's more? They don't feel one bit bad about it.

Give me a soothing roll on the ground, a good back scratch, ten minutes laying hooves up with the sun warm on my belly, and I am content. Donkeys know better than to overcomplicate life, and besides, when would we have the time?

Like any mother, I feel compelled to tell you about my offspring. Having given birth to two jennies and two jacks, I have, like humans, created some very special things myself. Unlike all humans but the enslaved, I said goodbye to them forever to continue my long walk in the service of these two-legged, highly-pushy creatures.

I have been walking all of my too-long life.

Humans have blossomed and withered as my feet have wandered through the gardens in which they grow and cast their seed. Before I arrived in Nazareth twelve years ago from my life on the trade routes, I rarely laid my head down for the night upon the same spot of earth. The stars overhead, consistent to my eyes, sometimes shone so clearly, their light pulsing like breath. I only slumbered because tomorrow is always better received with a good sleep.

But oh, those stars! Something in me echoed when they shone so brightly.

I was frequently overloaded on these routes. All humans, even patient ones, do this when time, materials, and desperation greet each other in wonderment as if trouble is something new. "Oh, hello! It appears we've gotten ourselves into a bind. Fancy that!"

Believe me, it's nothing new. Believe me, most speedy solutions involve overloading something. Believe me, it's never fun for the overloaded ones and it's almost never actually our fault. Humans have occupied the earth for many millennia and despite their intelligence, have yet to learn that applying great amounts of force births even greater amounts of resistance. So they try applying more force and then wonder why things break.

Talk about stubborn.

Yet certain humans walk among the rest, and I think they're better, but I should. Humans who realize others feel pain, even animals, arise in our lives. And when we beasts of burden find a sympathetic soul, we bear our burdens straight and tall, not crouched and always waiting for the sharp spark of struck pain.

Like humans, donkeys pick their favorite person, and sometimes we are joined with someone we feel like we've known all of our lives. Even a life as long as mine.

Mary is my person.

MARY OF NAZARETH

If it's true that nothing good comes out of Nazareth, I clearly don't understand the meaning of the word "good."

ST.IS

~ 2 ~

If a smile erupts on the streets of Nazareth once a day, it's a good day. Thankfully, Nazareth is a small village that doesn't seem to cast its cantankerous net too wide. Yet Nazarenes, obedient to the rules as a source of pride and a rod to control, somehow managed to get it right on festival days when they remembered with good food, wine, and dance, that life is meant to be lived and enjoyed, and time is never borrowed, nor can it ever be.

For what is time to begin with?

Mary smiled, though. Mary laughed and sang. Mary told the best stories. Mary knew how to live. We both did. A girl and her donkey, we traversed the scrubby hillsides, sat in the sure shade of the bristly cedars, picked up stones and examined them. Sometimes she kept them and sometimes not, and why she chose which stones, I still have yet to figure out. She always showed them to me because I was her friend and she was mine, and that was what truly mattered.

Though dutied to my maiden's bidding, her light load and easy manner erased many prior days of harsh toil. When something amused Mary, the whole street knew. People cried, "You bray like that donkey."

"Why, thank you!" she always said, and continued about her business whether helping her mother at the village oven, fetching water for the animals in the stable, caring for the sick, or delivering food to the unclean.

Mary's smart about such things.

Bray we would, she and I together. And we should. All of us.

Especially out in the open air!

Bray good donkeys, bray good humans, just like Mary and Is. Bray your songs and stamp your feet in the fresh air and sunshine. Feel the goodness of rain and grain. Pull and haul and carry when you must, think your lofty and mostly unnecessary thoughts, but always roll inside your celebrations, strange rituals, and the people in front of you who love you. And having done so, recall why you do all of this.

"Why do we?" a human might ask.

Because it pleases the Creator to see the created ones experiencing joy and loving one another.

Even donkeys know that's the point.

We entered the vicinity of Bethlehem on slow, crowded roads surrounding Jerusalem. Zion overflows with people arriving to celebrate Sukkoth (Sue-kuth), their harvest feast, as well as to be counted for the Caesar's census. Listen to Is: a bountiful harvest should always be celebrated before the worry about next year's begins.

I guard the door of the stable. In the clear night, stars dance in clusters and great trails of heavenly light foams into the darkened dome in the same thrilling display hanging there ever since I can remember.

A very tired Mary appears suddenly older, more present to the aches and pains this world offers. I watch and I wait. It's all I can do.

HOW WE GOT TO BETHLEHEM

We got to Bethlehem
the same way any of us
get anywhere, one hoof
in front of the other.

ST.IS

~ 3 ~

Mary learned young to spin yarn and work the loom. Some days, she led me to the fields to load up my baskets with freshly shorn wool. Out in the morning sun, she would circle her arms around my neck, place her cheek on mine, and squeeze with a squeal of delight. "I love you, Old Issy."

That's what Mary called me. Old Issy.

Some nights, Mary snuck out when fulsome stars flattered a low and golden moon, and we'd sit at the edge of the vineyard together, eating grapes. I would settle down so Mary might lean against me.

"There's one in every family," is an ancient saying I suspect will always be true. In the family of Joachim the elder and his wife Anna, Mary became that one.

Though kind and forgiving, like me, Mary learned to stand her ground. With brothers like hers, it isn't any wonder. But like any decent being, I'll let those two, Eli and Joachim the younger, speak for themselves.

Listen up.

About thirteen years after her birth, Mary, having placed fresh hay in the manger, came upon her brother Joachim in the stable yard. His exasperation at my homeward pace revealed his highly mistaken belief that working a beast for an entire, sweltering day without water is the perfect way to ensure a quick frolic home.

He flailed my thighs the entire way back from the fields where the family kept their goats. "Go faster, you idiot!"

Whack!

Don't let anybody fool you that we get used to being struck. We don't. Nothing does. Understand?

We came to the stable yard, the water trough full and ready for us. I was one of four.

"You will not drink tonight in punishment for being such a belligerent ass," Joachim said.

You don't even know the meaning of the word.

But what else could a donkey do? I followed him to my bed in the stable. I'd gone longer without water, most certainly. Donkeys aren't like camels, but we perform better on less food and water than horses. Say what you will about their beauty, but who will get things done in the least expensive manner possible?

Donkeys. That's who. When you want a job done right, you want an ass.

Mary set down the jar, rushed over on stiff legs, arms swinging like swords at her side. "No!"

"Oh, here she is. The Big Girl, come to take charge of a man's job." Joachim sneered without looking at her.

"You're only two years older than I am, Joachim. And if you're bent on doing a terrible job of taking care of living creatures, then yes, I will take charge."

"What if I say no?"

"What if I tell father you'll put a donkey out of commission eventually and then where will we be? What if that?"

He crossed his arms over his skinny chest. "You would dare?"

"Oh, brother." Mary laughed, placed a hand on each of his crossed forearms and with a little "Hmph!" pushed him to the side. "Keep talking, Joachim, all right? Come on, Issy—" she took my harness, "I've got more water than you can drink in a week."

"I'll tell father!" Joachim said as she passed him.

Mary turned, raised up on tiptoes and looked her brother in the eye. "Go right ahead."

The next day, Mary set my baskets on me. She sang a tune as we shuffled down the road. Relief filled me whenever Mary needed me, but I never knew to even hope for her words that day. "I need you now, Old Issy. I'm going to do whatever I can to keep you with me. I will find a lot of ways to need your help for a good while until everyone just assumes you're coming with me. Is that alright?"

I brayed, happy. Everybody knew when Mary gave her word, she would never go back on it. When Mary said, "Yes," she meant yes.

And Joachim could go jump in the Sea of Galilee.

JOE

I have found the greatest trait in a human being to be the ability to hold their tongue. Perhaps, like me, they've heard enough and seen enough it's left them tongue-tied, too. Sometimes life is so flabbergasting it leaves some of us gabber-fasting

ST.IS

~ 4 ~

"There go Mary and Issy. Two of a kind," the people in Nazareth liked to say. I didn't know specifically where our pairing was headed when young Joseph Ben Jacob rolled into Nazareth. He had moved to the city of Sepphoris to work his trade. Herod the Great, an Idumean not being of Israel, invested in the city's welfare as a place where surely the Messiah that was always being thrown in his face was very unlikely to emerge. He had no time for a Messiah, but as a man given to jealous fits about his throne, he had much time for the *idea* of a Messiah. So he built in Sepphoris much like he did all around Israel to remind its citizens how great a king they *already* had. A fine treasury was erected in the city as well.

Who needs a Messiah when Herod is so busy, busy, and busy being busy?

See what I mean about busy humans?

Joe, a young stone carver, had come to Sepphoris with his father to learn finer skills. When a cave-in occurred upon the failure of a load-bearing wall, many of the workers were dismissed for the afternoon, Joe included, in order to dig out the buried and clean up the site.

Eventually, Joe and Mary collided. And you should know, I take credit for the whole thing.

Donkeys see things humans do not as the prophet Balaam attested. Dogs do too; for how many times have canines been caught staring at an empty corner, communicating with their eyes, their mouths and their tails, someone the human cannot see?

Do people call the dog crazy? No.

Do they beat the dog for seeing such things? No.

Dogs' eyes and donkeys' eyes are much the same.

That day, a group of heavenly beings stretched across the path in front of us. One's hand stretched before us, light beams spreading out like a glowing glass wall. Of course I stopped! Happens all the time.

And humans think we're just stubborn.

A relaxed Mary was fighting sleep above the gentle rhythm of my gait. I didn't mind taking it slow. I'm not crazy.

Her brothers fought the night before inviting everyone to the uproar. And people say my voice sounds terrible! Finally, my maid slipped into the stable just before dawn's first light and curled up next to me whispering, "And people say you're a jackass, Issy. They've never met my brothers."

If I ever spoke again it would be to tell the world a female donkey is not a jackass. She's a jenny. Males are jackasses.

Not Joe, however.

Fatefully enough, Joe was gaining on foot from my right rear quadrant when a dozing Mary nodded too far forward and slipped off my back as I respected the wall of light. He dove forward, beating her to the ground. Her forehead collided with the back of his right shoulder. No face down in the dirt for Mary. Joe saw to that. His face didn't have the same luck.

The heavenly beings faded, most likely glad for an easy assignment.

The two laughed together as she climbed off of his back, regained a solid ground, shook the dust from her gown, and took my harness. He wiped the dirt from his face, leaving a dark streak down the middle of his forehead.

"I'm not sad you fell off of that donkey, maid," he said.

Mary whispered as they stood next to my ear, "I'm not either."

So wildly inappropriate!

I loved them for it.

"Who's this sweet beast?" Joe asked, still striped, still unaware of it.

"This is Issy. She's everything to me these days."

He reached out and scratched behind my ears. That's a good human being right there. "Do you have a family?"

"I do. They're a cantankerous lot. I get tired of their whining and complaining and fighting. Nothing is ever good enough, so you know what?"

"What?" His tone made clear he thought every word from her mouth was not to be missed. He helped her onto my back by interlacing his fingers and giving her foot a boost.

She steadied herself with a hand on his arm. "I'm going to live my life differently. I swear it ... What's your name?"

"Joe."

"I'm Mary."

Joe's eyes widened. "Are there many Marys in Nazareth?"

"What do you think, Joe?"

"That I know better than to even ask?"

"I'll let you be the judge of your own intelligence."

"Is your father Joachim?"

"Yes, he is!" Her eyes grew to the same size as his.

Their mouths dropped open.

"Are you Joseph Ben Jacob?" Mary asked.

"I am he."

He grinned, both he and Mary now oblivious to his forehead. Betrothed four years previously when Mary was only eleven years old, here they were, meeting for the very first time since they were children! Some would say it was by accident, but I knew better. And when a donkey knows, she knows for good.

Seeing angels helps, too.

Of course, more unexplainable events followed. And even more after that. Many times I wished their backs held burdens as easily as mine, but all I could do was remain close, help out when needed, and guard them like I am doing tonight. Although now, there are three of them. One, two, three.

And the third one is screaming his head off.

MARY AND HER BROTHERS

Humans name it instinct as if we are
completely unconscious of what we do over
and over. Perhaps it is instinctive, but it would
be a mistake to think it goes unrecognized,
that our actions, somehow predetermined by
what we are, hold little for us but their
completion. We learn just like everything else
does. We just know it begins somewhere deep
inside us.

ST.IS

~ 5 ~

Mary's brothers didn't care Joe was her right, legal, and just betrothed one. He was suspect of anything they might dream up.

Joe came from Bethlehem, the City of David— King David, the famous man after God's own heart. Mary's brothers scoffed.

"Those Bethlehemites think they're better than everyone else," Eli said one day on the way to the well.

And just go ahead and load up Old Is. One more day won't kill me.

Minutes later, Joachim pulled the bucket up from the depths. "Those tektons think they've got so much more to offer than the rest of us do."

Joe spoke moderately in all ways, truthful at all times, kindly whenever and if ever possible.

"He's like the weakest of women. His spine is made of mud," Joachim said that evening to Mary as they watched Joe walk toward them, his gait open and relaxed.

To donkeys, that sort of thing is called humility, but don't mind us, Joachim.

The truth about Joe didn't actually matter. They refused to like him. Had he been just like them, they wouldn't have noticed. Mary knew that. And, like all women who find a good man, she didn't care at all what her brothers thought.

Each evening he came, for their betrothal would become marriage as soon as Mary entered her childbearing years. Each morning following, Mary woke up professing one more thing to love about him.

Eli approached her one morning as she readied me.

Mary, by this time, had developed a reputation for weaving a good strong cloth from fiber she carded from fleece grown by the family flock and spun into wool. She ran her industry start to finish, capable of beginning-to-end production. She had just learned to weave a seamless garment used by rabbinical students. That day I was to accompany her to the fields. I loved the days Mary needed me.

"He's strange, Mary. We don't like him," Eli said the next morning as she adjusted my baskets.

"I really don't care, Eli."

"Well, you should know."

"And you should know, both you boys, that what is done is done. This is a family matter and whether or not you like him isn't something I care about and do you know why?"

Joachim crossed his arms over his chest.

There he goes again.

Forgive me, but I have noticed a phenomenon of wise brother/foolish brother over the centuries. I'll leave who is who to anyone's guess, though.

"I'd love to hear," Eli said in the same tone long lines seem to bring out in humans.

"Because everybody in this family hates everything about everyone, so I would say your opinion is suspect right from the start. Anybody would think God is doing a horrible job if they listened to you."

"You think you're so holy." Joachim grabbed her upper arm.

I stepped forward.

"Oh, and what are you going to do about it, jackass?"

See?

It's jenny, sir!

He swiped back a hand bent slightly at the knuckles and swung it across the left side of my face. Joachim is strong. I brayed, the high-pitched squeak then guttural cry accompanying Mary as she lunged at him, her hands flying forward like birds of prey into the feathers of his hair. She screamed as he toppled back and she went with him to the ground.

"Stop it, you two!" Eli, the largest of the family yelled, grabbing Mary by the neck of her gown and her belt and lifting her off. "What is the matter with you, Joachim?"

He set Mary on her feet. "And you! Mary, what has gotten into you? You act like you think you're so much better than we are."

"Yeah." Joachim stood, brushing down his robe. "As if you're so holy, so righteous, such a bright a star in God's heaven that nothing exists beyond you."

I had to give him credit for trying a little harder with the whole star picture. Then again, after all these years, I find hope whenever and wherever I possibly can. Maybe not probably. But possibly.

This could have been a fluke.

Mary raised a finger to his face, pushed out a sound, then snapped her hand back. "No. Come on, Issy. Come on."

She pulled me out of the stable yard and into the lane.

We walked twice as slowly on our way to the sheep. Mary calmed with each step, and soon a large flock of starlings, dipping and rising, coalescing and dissipating only to be drawn back into formation, took her attention. "I love that," she whispered. "How do they know, Issy?"

Animals just do.

Humans call it *instinct* as if we are completely unconscious of what we do over and over. Perhaps it is instinctive, but it would be a mistake to think it goes unrecognized, that our actions are a constant surprise. We learn just like everything else does. We just know it begins somewhere deep inside us.

We walked further along—people working, wheels turning, orders being barked, a baby crying, and somewhere someone was roasting meat and onions.

It turned into a good day after all.

"Joseph is so nice, isn't he, Issy?" Mary began her daytime opining about how kindly *he* spoke to her, not like her brothers. About the glow in his gaze when she spoke to him. How handsome she thought him with his quick brown eyes and infectious smile. I carried a young lady with love in her heart and hope picking up the weight of her worries from her mind and lifting it to God, who could actually do something about it.

"My beloved is mine. He was already mine, Issy. Isn't that wonderful?"

Happy for my maid, I dipped my head in a nod and did what I had been doing for fourteen hundred years. I kept my mouth shut and nestled my nose into her hand.

MARY AND SIMON

While humans don't know if God answers the prayers of donkey, I do know God's ears have heard mine, for does not the Creator of all know the deepest prayers of all hearts? How can it be otherwise?

ST.IS

~ 6 ~

Call me the practical sort, but naturally I should become so after all my trading and traveling. This region, this land of Israel, isn't new to me. I have lived in it more years and passed through it more times than I can recall. From Egypt up to the Silk Road and all that the East held for the West and the West desired from the East went right through it.

All upon my back, it seems.

And don't forget about all the wars. I have fought with the Canaanites, the Greeks, the Romans, the Babylonians, the Parthians, and the Israelites. And I have fought against the Canaanites, the Greeks, the Romans, the Babylonians, and the Parthians, but I have yet to fight against Israel. The Most High has preserved me to bear the Messiah, and you cannot bear that which you would destroy. I am a very good fighter, but best of all—

—I *am* a donkey mother, and we're noted in the animal kingdom for our good parenting. And please, don't take my word for that. Yes, these Nazarenes act as if they are so much more intelligent and experienced than I am.

How little they actually know about their lowly beast of burden. I have been to Jiuzhou, bells upon my harness and fine colors draped over my sturdy back. I have worked in mines and mills and on farms and building sites. Solomon's temple? Carried stone, I did. Several times I glimpsed the gates of death, only to be delivered before the clear waters of the trough and sweet clover.

On one of those peculiar days not to be forgotten, I caught view of donkeys like me when caravanning through the wilderness between Egypt and Ethiopia. These wild donkeys ran upon rocks and between brush down to the trickling bed of a river that rushes in spring. Braying and running and rolling down by the river that rushes in spring.

What I could be if free!

Let it be so!

While humans don't know if God answers the prayers of donkeys, I do know God's ears have heard mine, for does not the Creator of all know the deepest prayers of all hearts? How could it be otherwise?

The Creator was well on the way to answering my most practical of prayers, that Mary would be cared for and allowed to live in as much freedom as possible. Women and donkeys share many things common. We tend to take on weight so others might do as they want, or will, and sometimes, yes, should.

On a morning she could spare, Mary asked her cousin, an expansive, booming young man named Simon, to accompany us to the pasture. Halfway there, she stopped us. "Look, Simon," she whispered, laying a hand on his arm. "I actually need an escort. Will you go with me to Sepphoris? I want to see the kind of work Joe does."

Simon, not nearly as congealed in grievance as her brothers, laughed, his eyes sparking as if struck with flint. "Oh, yes! This will be our adventure."

I liked Simon, always ready for something new, always on the lookout for happy times and things to enjoy. One of the best humans I knew at simply being a human, he tended not to overcomplicate things.

Humans love complications.

That morning's journey took us almost two hours, the roads crowded with supplies being hauled into the city.

"I don't want Joe to see us if at all possible. He might think I'm spying on him," Mary said. We stepped through the gates of the city, passing spacious villas in which Greeks and Romans, priests and the wealthy, lived in style.

"You *are* spying on him, right?"

Mary jumped on his uncertainty. "Well, I like to think of it as making sure of a few things. I don't think it's strange a woman wants to see the man she's going to marry working, and working when he doesn't know she's watching. She could find out so much about him, don't you think?"

"That's still spying."

"Oh, all right, Simon! I'm spying on him."

The bantering continued.

Don't say a word, Is.

Joe saw us right away. He laughed when Mary confessed her reason for being in the city as soon as we were caught. More importantly, he scratched the top of my head as they spoke.

"I'll show you some parts of the site, Mary."

She turned to Simon. "See? It's all working out."

Simon whispered in my ear. "She's a sneaky spy, isn't she?"

Joe rendered decorative carvings and was learning the art of the mosaic. Even I knew they were beautiful. "My father brought me here to find work and get more experience," Joe said. "He had to go home last year after my uncle became ill and died. My uncle was in our care for many years. He was my mother's brother, curled up and on his side. But we all loved him. It crushed my mother. So here I am by myself."

Joe's work, carving capitals for the tops of the pillars formed to surround a villa's courtyard, was refined and bore a lightness that any sculptor would appreciate.

Good for him! Good for Mary!

I worked on many cities over the years, and Sepphoris, a showpiece, wealthy and cosmopolitan, proved the old saying there are no details too small for those who can afford them. That a tekton so young could already carve to this level was rare.

"No wonder they kept you on after your father went back to Bethlehem," Simon said. "You're really good, Joe."

"Thanks, Simon."

That evening when we entered the stable yard with Joe who walked back with us, Mary's brothers jeered and jabbed at him with their words. But Joe and Mary only looked at one another.

And at me sometimes.

Don't ever forget about Old Is. I like attention as much as anybody.

Unless a baby is born. Babies should always get to shine their new and heavenly light. Don't ever forget this either. *Is* will stand her ground to keep that baby safe. Just like I'm doing tonight.

A YEAR OF PEACE

True love will walk away if
you tell it you don't want it.
That's just the way it is. But it
will never stop loving you.
That's just the way that is, too.

ST.IS

~ 7 ~

A year passed. Mary greatly matured under the light of love, Joe improved as a tekton, the brothers still outshone me mightily for the title of Israel's Top "Jackass," and I accompanied my maiden everywhere. It was the most beautiful, peace-filled, and companionable year of my life. I started looking upon Mary as my human child not long into our friendship. After all, she took me with her on her jaunts and I offered her more years of experience than she could ever comprehend. I decided the day she led me to that trough, standing between me and a much bigger and stronger Joachim, I would protect her as my jennie. Her becoming a married woman wouldn't stop me from a decision like that.

"You worship that donkey!" Joachim said over and over.

"You sound like the Emperor." Mary tossed her head.

"Donkey worshipper."

"Roman! Would we would all pay taxes to you!"

Eventually, Mary ignored him. "He's getting tiresome, Issy. I'm going to be very excited to go live with Joe."

Not that it stopped him from taunting her, but nobody in the family ever accused Joachim of understanding subtleties.

That year, Joe called on Mary almost every evening and we sat together. Despite the walk to Sepphoris each morning, Joe took a home in Nazareth, just down the lane. Mary never went to Joe's house, of course, but it didn't help it was nicer than Mary's.

"That, Joe," Eli said whenever Mary mentioned anything about moving in after the wedding. "He's just a show off."

"At least he has something to show off, Eli," said Mary.

"I work hard, Mary."

"Yes, you do. And think how much more everyone would appreciate that if you didn't try to bring Joe down into your own jealous world. He's doing what his father did and is successful in his own right. What else would you have him do?"

"Become a rabbi. He is smart," Eli conceded.

"Well..." Mary looked up at the sky in consideration, "maybe he is one. Maybe he just speaks of God and the law in different ways."

"You speak as if we're all rabbis, then." Eli squinted and shook his head with a grimace for accompaniment.

Mary shrugged.

"You're so strange, girl."

Thank you for the compliment.

How strange was soon to unveil itself.

Mary's parents discussed and planned the upcoming wedding, which was only three months away. Anticipation and infatuation won over any sense of administration on the part of Mary and Joe. Though a great blessing to be espoused in a good arrangement, add the love in their hearts, and it was doubly wonderful.

"I feel so blessed to have you, Joe," she said to him many times over the course of the year.

To such words Joe never failed to reply, "I am the one who is chiefly blessed in you, Mary."

That strange night was almost as glorious as this one now that the baby has finally stopped crying, thank the good Lord. Seeing this outcome was impossible at the time, but any outcome of great magnitude usually is. But right now, Mary, like any woman who has just given birth, is inside the house getting cleaned up after her labor. Joe, not knowing what to do with the baby while she's gone, has laid him the manger!

Oh, dear. He'll learn soon enough, won't he?

This has been a very long night for us all.

MARY AND GABRIEL

I know my archangels.
And my archangels
know me.

ST.IS

~ 8 ~

One December evening, a few months before the wedding, Joe accepted an invitation to sleep in Sepphoris. "We fell behind because of that cave-in. Unfortunately, the merchant we're working for doesn't understand why that should make a difference as to when the project is finished." He shrugged. "I hate to say it, Mary, but these things happen, and quite regularly."

Mary, having just finished a seamless garment for her cousin Andrew, a new student of a rabbi near Hebron, was just as glad for an early night.

"I'm sleeping with Issy," she informed her parents after the December evening meal. Mary didn't bed down with me in the stable. We quit the property altogether, down to a grove of cedar trees just at the edge of town where her aunt and uncle's barley field, shorn for the year, was scheduled to be left fallow for a while.

"You know what, Issy?" she said as we walked along, "I don't know how I get away with this wandering." She shrugged and sighed. "Maybe it's because I'm trying to make an occupation for myself." We walked a bit more. "Do you ever wonder what it's like in those grand villas in Sepphoris?"

Not one bit.

I had been owned by several influential people. The villas of Sepphoris sounded like a terrible life. No rolling around and scratching allowed. No, thank you!

"Sometimes I do. But then—" she hugged me around the neck, "—I would never be free like I am now. Nobody would think to rob the likes of us. Besides, I have you to protect me, and Joe will be joining us soon. Or rather, I guess we will be joining him. And then, well, perhaps we won't be able to wander like we do, but it won't matter will it? Because we'll all be loved."

Over the years a lot of proverbs have been spoken in my presence and I stand by my keen observation that it truly is better to be in a simple home with love than a palace without it. To be fair, however, one good year in Alexandria I served a wealthy priest's kind son. Love makes all the difference to any given situation. I may be just a beast, but I know that much.

Joe was preparing a fine home for his beloved and she deserved it. Mary deserved to receive all she had ever given to me. I was as free as a donkey could be given the time and place I found myself. A lot of food. A lot of fresh water. A lot of hugs. And even some rolling around.

Protection. Companionship.

Oh, do not let our wandering days be done, sweet maid.

I sat down and Mary curled up next to me. When she fell asleep, I fell asleep, too. It seemed like only a nod when a great light startled us both.

It swirled and sparkled into a form as brightly terrifying and as magnificently beautiful as any angel I had seen before. Before it spoke, I knew this was no regular messenger angel, no unnamed helper angel of which a profusion exists more than any of us can fathom. No, this was an archangel.

And I know my archangels.

The Most High sent Gabriel?

My, my!

Mary scrambled to a sitting position, her neck craned back at the sight of eternal meeting mortal, of the usually unseen and yet much wondered about materializing right in front of us. From ghostly thin to rivaling even the Lighthouse at Alexandria, Gabriel shone a fierce and flaming love.

"Hello, Mary. You are full of grace. God is with you." His angelic voice met my ear directly as if the waves of sound needed no travel, only recognition.

Mary gasped. This being talked! He knew her name! And he was speaking to her! Her body stiffened as her hands covered her opened mouth.

Gabriel knelt down on one knee in front of her. "You don't have to be frightened, Mary. God has seen you and is pleased with you."

She curled her spine and relaxed it against me.

Good girl.

"You're going to conceive a son through the Holy Spirit and name him Jesus."

What? My Mary? Conceiving through the Holy Spirit? What does that mean? What could that entail? And how does this even work?

She stiffened again as her ears received heaven's announcement.

"He will be great and will be called the Son of The Most High."

That sounded better. A great son? Of The Most High?

I bowed my head. I know this Most High. All the animals do. We are not the ones who have forgotten, so don't ever think that. Don't ever think that.

"God will give him his father David's throne and he'll be the king of the people of Jacob forever. And his kingdom won't end."

"How?" said Mary. "I've never been with a man."

Gabriel reached out. "The Holy Spirit will come on you, Mary, overshadowing you with the power of The Most High. Because of this, the baby will be called God's Son."

God's Son. The promised one? Could it be the Messiah who was promised to me?

Oh, let it be so!

Centuries and centuries ran through my mind like the blur of a chariot and the vision of a vast plain of grasses and streams and room to run took over. And I breathed in the smell of the free wind blowing through my mane, down my flanks, and across my knobby old knees. To sit and sit and sit, my back never to bow under the weight of mankind again …

Oh, what a day that will be!

Gabriel continued, slicing through my thoughts with his news. "Even your cousin Elizabeth is pregnant though she's advanced in age. She was finally able to conceive and is in her sixth month right now."

Elizabeth had been praying for years for a child. Why God kept her womb closed was fodder for family gossip.

"God's Word always does what it proclaims," Gabriel said.

Mary drew in breath after breath.

56

What she was thinking or feeling I couldn't pretend to guess. Who can know what a proclamation such as that would do to a maid?

Hello, there! God wants to have a Son here on earth and you won! You get to be his mother. You'll go though a process that, in all honesty, is only explained in very general terms bringing with it a heavy sack filled with questions like, will it hurt? Will it burn? What will it be like to walk around with God's Son inside my body? Will he be bigger and more developed? Will he come out talking? Oh, dear, what if he comes out talking? How will Joe and I provide what a future Messiah needs? Questions abound to which there are as yet no answers, but there will be! You can be sure of that!

And then.

Oh, and then.

I could barely think about it.

The shame inherent to such a situation! For who would believe her? Would she even tell them the truth? I have witnessed a lot of strange truths but this situation, when explained, felt like the most outlandish excuse I had ever heard.

Mary didn't answer right away. I can assure you a strong young woman like Mary sat on her heels for about a minute and thought about it. What if she refused? Would she be struck down? Mary knew the scriptures enough to know people were struck down for less.

Oh, Mary! I wished I knew what she was thinking. *Don't forget the first piece of news that God is pleased with you!*

My Mary was a pleasure to God with or without her answer. Can there be better news? *There's nothing to be afraid of*, he said. Remember Mary? Nothing!

Mary straightened her shoulders and looked up at Gabriel, raising to her knees. "I'm God's servant. Yes. May all that you said happen, just as you say it will."

Gabriel lowered his head, reached out both hands, and placed them atop our heads. The love, strength, and regard from him sang into us. I felt as if he was saying, "Sometimes I don't know how you Earth creatures do it." And he smiled at us.

I brayed and brayed and brayed!

And Mary shushed me and laughed.

Gabriel's smile never faded as he turned back into the brightest of light that collected itself into a blinding ball and zipped off into the darkness.

His knee print remained on the dry ground. Mary reached out and placed a hand in its middle. "It's warm, Issy!"

She turned to me, eyes glowing like amber, the light of the holy shining onto and into us.

"Oh, Issy! It's true! The Messiah is finally coming. The promises were true!"

I brayed a hallelujah and enjoyed a good roll in the knee print of an archangel.

And here we stay in Bethlehem, the first leg of this journey complete. And here we abide in a stable no less, exhausted amid a crowd of tired animals who journeyed here just like we did. Donkeys and horses, not to mention a beautiful red heifer curled near the manger refusing to leave even though Joe has nudged him with his foot several times. A baby still lays in that manger, wrapped in cloths, because Joe fell asleep right there in the hay.

Oh, good. Mary comes. She is a mother now. I trust her to be a good one. Able to stand up to older brothers for me, imagine what she will do for her own child? She lays a hand atop my back. "Well, friend. The angel was right, wasn't he?"

I squeak the first note of my bray as quietly as I can and she circles her arms around my neck and squeezes. "You were here. I'm so glad, my dear Old Issy."

I am happier than I have ever been, here on this night, with only the stable in which to dwell and bear children. Namely, Jesus. We usher in our Messiah and praise God, The Most High, who seems to favor secret work in ways almost nobody ever suspects ahead of time.

Men approach.

"Oh, my!" Mary says. "What in the world do they want?"

It's quite unbelievable, but a group of shepherds are walking toward the stable. I can smell them from here.

MARY PONDERS

Having been forced to follow the twists and turns of humanity, I can assure you things get complicated when they rush forward in their own might to carve their path. They know this but somehow always think they are the exception to the rule. Perhaps someday ...

ST.IS

~ 9 ~

Mary sagged against me soon after Gabriel left, falling into a deep sleep. How and when the Holy Spirit came upon her, I cannot say. She never discussed it in my presence with anyone and I cannot even imagine such a thing.

Joe continued his stay in Sepphoris for the next two days with plans to attend the Sabbath meal with Mary's family. Mary waited, of course; what else could she do? She shied from the family fray. We made camp each day in the vineyard, her distaff, spindle and freshly cleaned wool in my baskets. We sat by the vines, branches spreading over us, shading us from the high sun, and she worked the wool, preparing it for the loom.

"Of course, Issy"—she attached a white blossom of fleece to the distaff—"I have no idea what Joe will say. I'm nervous. I never thought ... I mean. Who can even imagine something like this is even possible?"

She pulled at a pinch of fleece, twisting the filaments together. When enough of it lengthened to wrap securely around the spindle, she paused. "You do know life will be different for us, don't you? Do you think he will believe me?"

I squeaked. I wanted to tell her although people come and people go, donkeys stay forever as long as we're wanted. And I wouldn't forsake her, no matter what Joe decided.

"You're right. He's a good man. Whatever he does it won't be because he didn't think about it." She began twisting again. "I don't want to think about it."

I don't blame you, Mary. How does a human consider the impossible?

After attaching the thread to the spindle, she twisted it, the spindle weighing down the resulting yarn as we sat together in the shade, waiting and waiting. For two days her tension pricked at my ears. Held down like a bottle in water, every so often a bubble of panic rose to the surface. Nobody bothered us in the vines. No proclaiming angels. No disdaining brothers. Nothing but a young woman and her donkey resided, holding a private court for an unseen, young judge who held her future in his hands. Plans once so secure, so perfect, now sat upon a sharp summit, capable of rolling in three-hundred-and-sixty-odd directions from a tipping completely beyond her control.

She worked several hours then stood to stretch her legs and roll her shoulders.

"We can either believe God's promises or not, Issy. And all I know is, when I choose to do so, I feel courage inside of me. When I don't—" she hushed to a whisper, "I'm so afraid I don't know what to do."

I wanted to tell her God always keeps promises if we allow for it. And even if we don't, even if we think God waited too long to make a move, The Most High still works on our behalf. Having been forced to follow the twists and turns of humanity, I can assure you it's definitely more complicated when they rush forward in their own might to carve their own path without the Lord.

Somehow, though, The Most High doesn't waste any of it and that's one of the reasons God is so great.

And now here we watch the night deepen yet more as shepherds file into the stable, at least seven in total.

"He's in the manger! The baby is in the manger!" one of them says, younger than the rest, eyes glowing like aged wood and skin browned more deeply than the others. His words soar with a wonder extravagant from the mouth of a lowly shepherd.

"Obviously, Nathan," the oldest of the group scolds, nervous, perhaps, at being in town in such crowded conditions. Who knew how long they had been out in the fields?

Joe grabs his staff and gains his feet. I could almost hear his thoughts: *Just as we were all getting a rest.*

"It's like the angel said, Isaiah." Nathan turns. "Right there. Swaddled like a lamb."

"A spotless lamb." Isaiah nods. "My, Lord. I can hardly believe my eyes."

The rest shuffle behind Isaiah and Nathan. All stand at the manger. Several swipe at their tears. I have been in Israel long enough to know that a swaddled lamb means one thing and one thing only. Its perfection, its rarity,

63

means it is born only to die.

"May I?" asks the old man. "May I just touch him?"

Like Mary, he seems to be a true believer in God's promises.

This is truly the Messiah, isn't it?

I know it now. The shepherds being here speak to me, a low-born beast, humans of like cast. And they tell me I am not wrong.

Mary smiles and nods. "Gently. I don't want to wake him. He just stopped crying a little while ago."

Jesus stretches the way newborn babies do, a tiny foot releasing itself from the folds of cloth as if to say *yes, please go ahead.* Isaiah reaches out a hand and touches the top of Jesus's foot. The other foot slides out and he touches that one, too.

Joe rubs his eyes. "An angel you said?"

We seem to collect angels, the three of us. But that's what happens in the service of The Most High.

Mary lies down in the straw. Joe lifts the baby from the manger and hands him to his mother. She holds him close in the crook of her arm, his little head resting in the hollow of her wing. "An angel?" she asks, too.

Yes. Tell us about your angel.

"Not just *an* angel, although one did speak," Nathan said, taking a knee so the men behind him could see. "There was a whole host of them. Praising God! Right Isaiah?"

"That's right." The older shepherd joins his young compatriot, down on a knee. "What's that fella's name?"

Jesus!

I bray instead. All heads swivel toward me at the noise. So I toss my head as I turn toward the stars and the night and the moon and the way the wind picks at the leaves of the nearby olive trees, at the neighbor's house, and the tender light of oil lamps shining through windows. Soft conversations seep into the atmosphere like clouds of warmth into the sea of life. All of creation seems to be making its presence known right here in this moment.

Including me.

"It's Jesus," says Joe.

"Jesus? Well, um, uh," says Nathan. "I was expecting—"

Mary laughs. "What? What were you expecting?"

Nathan blushes. "Hassan? Hezekiah?"

All the people laugh together.

Nathan ducks under his hands. "I mean, the angel did say he was the Son of The Most High."

Mary leans forward and places a hand on his arm. "It's all right, Nathan. We've all thought the same thing. I bet even my sweet little Issy over there did."

Bray I do.

"Issy! Shhhhh," says Mary, still smiling.

I stomp my front hooves and dance a little instead. One of the shepherds runs his hand along my spine as if to gently calm me. But Jesus sleeps on.

I think he might be the type of human that sleeps through anything, although it's probably too soon to tell.

JOE FINDS OUT

Some stories are too strange to be spun in the mind of a mortal.

ST.IS

~ 10 ~

Joe met us in the vineyard.

"Mary!" He hurried forward and took her hand. "It seems like it's been forever."

She gripped his hand, both sets already worn from work with stone and wool and tools and the materials of life. She squeezed hard, pressing back three days worth of anguish.

"What's the matter?" he asked as her eyes closed.

"Oh, Joe!" She opened them. "I don't even know how I'm going to explain this. And I doubt you're even going to believe me when you hear. It's that crazy."

He sat her down in the shade of a blue evening just losing its grip on the thin warmth of the winter day. Mary pulled me near and rested her hand on my neck for comfort. The sky displayed varying shades of plum and violet stacked like folded linen before a crimson veil the color of Mary's aching heart.

"Tell me, Mary. You can tell me anything. You know that."

"Joe ..."

I pressed my nose into her hand.

She took a deep breath. "Do you believe angels are real?"

What kind of a question is that?

"I've never seen one, Mary. I guess I've always thought angels appear to special people. You know, those who are called by God to do things so important an angel needs to make that perfectly clear."

"So you do?"

"Yes. You could definitely say that."

"All right." Another deep breath steadied her as her hand found the top of my head, her fingers curling around my ear, drawing up to the top, and down again. She continued this as she spoke. "I saw an angel the other day."

"You did? Mary that's amazing! Are you all right?"

"I truly am."

"What did the angel look like?"

I sagged in relief. If he didn't believe an angel came, he surely wouldn't believe the rest of her story. But we had a fighting chance now! The best thing would be to remain an *us*: Mary, Joe and Old Is.

"Bright and like a light. Fierce and beautiful. But not a bad fierce, Joe. It was a fierce you want on your side. A truth that sang even though the angel spoke in words."

"What did the angel say? Did it have a name?"

"Gabriel."

His hand flew to the top of his head and smashed down the curls that had escaped his head covering. "Gabriel?"

"Yes."

"Oh! Well ..."

"I know, Joe. I—"

"When was this?"

"Three nights ago."

Shock wiped his face clean as he tried to believe something while his brain instantaneously handed him all the reasons an angelic invitation couldn't be so. Love will do that to a person. But sometimes it's absolutely true and all it needs is time, no matter what the brain says otherwise.

"Tell me everything."

Mary imparted the news exactly as I remembered it. As she spoke, each word seemed to enter a place within Joe, gathering with the others that had tumbled down there already. And not just Mary's words, but all the other words he'd ever heard or read, for Joe wasn't only a learner of the written law, he was a keeper of the oral traditions of Israel.

Somehow, Joe let them fall into him as truth, for Joe, a just young man, believed God's promises were for his good. I had heard him say so several times. And love helped out too that day. It never fails when called upon.

"So, you said, yes." He took her hand. "Oh, Mary."

Even a donkey could see his head spinning with the undeniability of such a tale. It was too strange to be spun in the mind of a mortal, and so young and inexperienced a one at that.

"The Messiah? Are you certain that's what Gabriel said?"

"Completely."

Joe dropped his face into his hands, leaning into his own flesh as he looked up at his betrothed. "Well. All right. So." He slapped his hands on his thighs. "I have to think what to do." His hands found his face again.

"Please don't leave me, Joe. I have no idea how I'm going to tell—"

His head snapped up, eyes locking onto hers. "No. Don't. Don't tell your parents, Mary. That's going to end exactly like you think it will."

"You don't think—"

"Yes. I do."

"They're so *prideful*!"

"Everybody is, my love. But, yes, their way of showing it is more far-reaching than most people's."

They sat together in silence for a minute, a minute in which I could have traversed the Sahara and back for long how it felt. Finally Mary whispered, "Do you believe me? You do? Don't you?"

Joe sighed. "I do, Mary. God help us, and you, me, and the child, but I do."

"I'm so glad." She began to cry. "I have felt so alone, Joe."

Joe took her hand, covering it with the one that remained. "I'm here, Mary. I don't know what this means or how this is going to work."

"Do you mean we can still get married?"

He paused.

Oh, no. I tossed my head. *No, Joe. Please. Can't you see we need you?*

"Joe?"

"Mary. There's the law to consider. I don't know what I'm supposed to do about this. I don't think there's anything specifically written down for what a good Son of David does when his betrothed is carrying God inside of her."

I conceded to his common sense.

"I knew you wouldn't do anything rash!" Mary cried. "I'm so glad you're not going to just walk away, right now, right here. I don't know what else to expect, but yes, do what you have to do. Will you still come here in the meantime?"

"Yes, I will. I won't leave you to be alone in this. We'll have to figure out something."

"Joe."

"I know, Mary. I know. But it's the Messiah. Do you understand what this means?"

And I don't know if you'll believe me, but pure light, a kind of glory settled on, in and through him, and Joseph Ben Jacob praised the Living God. He sung of deliverance from the yoke of darkness, he sung of the light which pierces it, and he sung of hope in the Messiah, his Messiah, the Lord God's Christos. He sung of the anointing oil of the people come to the world, right here in Nazareth, in the womb of his beloved.

Joseph believed Mary only enough to praise God with all his heart, soul, mind, and strength.

The City of David sleeps. The animals finally settle in after the commotion of feminine cries, of blood, of tears, and of agony as new life bursts from a place much too small to give it easy passage. But it comes forth nonetheless and it says, "I am here."

The Messiah has come to light the world, good humans. He has come from the secret place of a young woman from Nazareth who risked her life to bring him to everyone.

Bray! And bray!

And never stop reminding your children that Jesus comes to tell the world how much God loves it, all of it, including lowly beasts like Is. From all of my years on this planet, I know God doesn't love donkeys more than anything else, but on a night like tonight, it sure does feel like it.

And if a tale is ever told, you can be sure my Mary is the one, the only one, that can tell in completion what has happened here tonight, how, and why. Not that anyone will truly give her credit for it. But if I know Mary, it won't matter. That the story lives and breathes will be enough for she who believes God's promises.

JOE HAS A PLAN

Humans plan and God laughs,
it's true. But God plans and
we donkeys say, "How long
will we be gone?"

ST.IS

~ 11 ~

Two days later, we walked with Joe to Sepphoris.

Along the way, we paused in a grove of sycamores to wait for a group of Roman soldiers passing through. Mary leaned against me, balling up her head covering in her right hand and kneading it with the other. "Joe, you've got to tell me what you've decided."

"Just give me a few more minutes, Mary. I promise when we get to Sepphoris I will lay it all out. Did you bring along your possessions?"

Mary nodded. She had loaded me with all of her spinning equipment, a few trinkets she had collected as relatives died off over the years, including a small box of healing salve her grandmother had made before she died a few years prior. The old woman had tucked it into Mary's hands and said, "Guard this. It's yours. It will heal, but I am trusting you not to waste it, Mary. Use it for those who desire it. That's how you will know who to give it to, do you understand?"

After the soldiers passed, we pulled back onto the roadway, the dust from the carts and wagons thick in my nostrils. The clinking of tools accompanied the percussion of hooves and feet, and someone whistled the miles away with us. Finally, having passed through the city gates and traveled by the villas, Joe led us to sit near a well.

"What are we doing here?" she asked.

"Simon is coming. Mary, he's taking you to your cousin Elizabeth's. You and Issy."

"Why?"

"From what Gabriel said, Elizabeth could use help and you need to get away from your family. After the birth of her baby, I will find a place for you to live quietly. You can have the baby and I will make sure you both will be all right."

"So our betrothal?" She held out her hand.

He took it, squeezed tenderly, then handed it back.

Tears filled her eyes.

"The law forbids it. There's nothing I can do. It's up to the father to take care of matters, but seeing this situation is unprecedented at best, this is the only solution I can come up with. Mary, it's the Messiah. I won't make you go through this alone, but I can't marry you. I just can't."

Mary gulped back a sob, calmed herself, then asked, "What will you tell my family?"

"It's already arranged. I will tell them tonight. As your betrothed I have every right to do this."

"What will be your reason for keeping this a secret?"

Joe took her hand. "Your family might be coarse, and they might be vindictive at times, and most definitely prone to think they know everything, Mary, but they're not stupid. They'll know I'm putting you into hiding for a time, and I think they'll know why. What they can't possibly figure out on their own, however, is that the child is of the Holy Spirit. And that—" he sighed heavily, "—is a message I'm not ready to deliver. I'm not even sure it's my right to do so."

Later, refusing to go into the inn with Simon, Mary held back her tears until that night in the stable. She curled up into my side and cried all night long.

Here we are in another stable, a young one curled up into the side of Mary. Our days for curling together are now done. Perhaps she might make her way to me of an odd evening and lay down and remember the good old days, and we'll breathe together like we always end up doing. But all young people grow up, don't they? They assume their positions in life and if a donkey is lucky, she's asked along for the ride.

The Messiah is sleeping, the shepherds entered their fields anew, and a star appeared on the horizon tonight that hadn't been there yesterday—as if its light had finally met the earth on the night the Light of the One Light came.

No braying now in the stillness, but my heart brays in joy and that is enough. My years are now numbered. His birth has brought my freedom and for that, I love him already.

I will carry the Messiah. Where, when, and why, I do not know. I only know that I know it will come to pass in one lifetime. One lifetime more? Seems like but a dream. But I know whose donkey I am, because I know whose donkey I have been since I was twelve years old.

I belong to the Master now.

MARY AND SIMON JOURNEY TO HEBRON

Humans, take note! Samson
didn't use one of our jawbones
for nothing. Personally speaking,
however, I would rather use mine
for speaking words of wisdom.
Hee-Haw!

ST.IS

~ 12 ~

Mary and Simon led me south from Sepphoris through treacherous curves where thieves and robbers awaited vulnerable travelers. Always at the ready, it should be more widely known, donkeys are good protectors. We fight with our front legs *and* our back legs. We have it coming *and* going.

However, even I knew that when God places the Promised One into a human being, God is fully capable of leading those feet in the way of peace.

Simon worried me far more than the possibility of highway bandits. Jumpy humans are always ready for a cliff tumble and there are some situations even a donkey can't get them out of.

"What was that?" he said for the twenty-fifth time, four days in and ten miles north of Jerusalem. "Did you see anybody behind that tree?"

"I didn't see anybody, Simon." Mary adjusted herself atop me. "Stop a second, Issy. I have got to walk some, stretch my legs a little."

I did. She slid right off.

Simon didn't know of her condition, by the way, and thank goodness. He possessed only two behaviors: playful and protective.

Overprotective.

And Mary, free on the inside, much preferred the fun side. Although both entertained me. Humans are truly the most amusing beings on the planet. They even put monkeys to shame if all you do is observe them.

She took my harness from Simon. "Stop worrying, Simon. If you look around every curve for danger, you're going to eventually come upon it."

He laughed. "That makes no sense. It's either there or it isn't."

She shrugged. "Remember the story of Balaam's ass? Nobody saw the angel but the donkey."

That's right! That is right!

"And that angel was there to hurt Balaam, but the donkey saved him."

She's right about that, too.

"I'm not following you, Mary." Simon joined step with her.

"Well, if that donkey could spot danger that nobody could see, imagine what Issy can do with what's in front of her? Right? Issy knows things, Simon. She's brilliant that way and will keep us safe because if we're safe, she is too."

Mary is brilliant.

"And besides that," she continued, "God is watching over us."

Simon puffed. "Yeah, right, Mary."

Mary started, dropping my reigns then swinging them back in her grasp. "What do you mean?"

"Like God really cared about us when Rome took over. I'll grant you the donkey, but God? I don't know anymore. I'm tired of carrying soldier packs a mile. I'm tired of bowing and scraping. I'm tired that we are all held in check with threats of being sold into slavery or killed. I don't know what's worse, obeying all these laws to keep God happy while, apparently, that's impossible, or taking my chances."

"Simon!"

"Listen, Mary, don't tell me you've never wondered."

Mary stayed silent.

"Really, Mary? I always thought you were honest with yourself."

"I am honest. You can't know everything about a person, Simon. You can't. Even me."

"You've doubted God?"

"Do I have to say it out loud?"

"Mary! Come on!"

"Yes! Okay, yes I have. Many times. But you know what, Simon? God is still with me even then. And look! Here we are! You and I together on this road. I love you and you love me and look, Issy is here, and we're heading to Jerusalem together."

"But Mary, at any moment—"

"But not this one. Not right now. You want to know something about me, Simon? You really do? Because you're not going to like it."

"Yes, I really do."

The family chin jutted forward on both of them.

"My life is always in the hands of either my father, or now, Joe. If I so much as make one misstep that could be it for me. So, maybe Rome has come and the foot of that oppressor Herod is on our necks, and maybe God *is* mad at us. I don't know. But between Herod, Rome, my father, and God? Right now, I'll trust God. That's my best option. I don't have the luxury of being my own best option like you do. It's been Rome for womenkind since Eve ate of the fruit. Now do you understand?"

"This whole world stinks," Simon said.

Mary raised a hand to her mouth. "It does. But its beauty will take your breath away, too. And it will get you through. At least it does for me. Do you ever just go outside and sit, Simon?"

"No."

"Well, you might want to try it sometime."

She's right. If it isn't the vineyard, it's that grove of sycamore trees north of town. There are all sorts of places that shall always remain a secret between Mary and me. If that little baby doesn't end up wandering around the countryside looking for things, I will be most surprised. And maybe Jesus will invite Old Is to join him sometimes.

Don't be jealous. It took me fourteen hundred years to get here.

MARY AND ELIZABETH

Oh, humans. My toil is easy compared to yours. I rise, I stand, I bear your burdens and when you lift them from my back, they are gone. But you, you carry your burdens day and night, shouldering them even when there are none, and taking them on when you might choose otherwise.

ST.IS

~ 13 ~

The one-hundred-mile trek took us a week, sleeping under the stars, observing the Sabbath at a relative of Joe's along the way. Finally, late one afternoon, having pushed our way through Jerusalem, we arrived in the hill country of Hebron, and finally to the home of Mary's older cousin, Elizabeth.

Mary, tired as any pregnant woman at the beginning of her pregnancy, leaned into Simon as she dropped from my back. "I'm glad to be here, Simon, aren't you?"

"I am. And I'm ready to see Andrew."

Andrew's escapades were only known to the younger generation.

Mary laughed. "Don't let him lead you too far into trouble, Simon. He's luckier than you are when it comes to that sort of thing. I hope he likes the garment I made for him!"

She peeked in Elizabeth's door. "Elizabeth?"

She stepped back.

"Mary! Cousin, you are here!" Joyful words escaped onto the street preceding her exit, belly first, through the doorway and into a shared embrace.

The women pulled away, clasped hands, looked into each other's faces, then embraced again, Mary leaning forward over the old woman's belly. Once again that light came. From within them both it escaped and embraced like long lost friends. The women began to weep. Their tears fell upon me like flower petals on the head of a wise and much beloved king.

It was joy. That's what it was.

Mary was so happy her cousin had finally received the favor of blessing humanity with her womb, and for being given the experience of becoming a mother.

And she could say the same for herself!

Elizabeth pulled back and that strange light filled her again as she spoke in a loud voice as if before a crowd of onlookers, not just Simon and a donkey. "You are blessed among all the women, and so is the baby you're pregnant with!"

How does she know?

Thank goodness nobody else heard! "But why am I so blessed that the mother of my Lord comes here?" She grabbed Mary's hands again. "As soon as I heard your greeting, Mary, my baby jumped for joy!"

Mary squeezed her hands and smiled.

"The Lord has kept his promises," Elizabeth continued, "and I am blessed for believing them."

Simon drew closer to my side then leaned in with a whisper. "I'm going to fill the trough for you, girl."

Bless you, good fellow.

Mary joined in with Elizabeth's proclaiming of God's goodness.

"Oh, Elizabeth, I feel like Hannah! My soul! It's as if God is so big inside of it, so full of joy my spirit rejoices too! It's true. God is our savior! The Lord looks kindly on even an everyday young woman like myself. He blesses me so greatly, people living generations from now will agree.

"And God's mercy even extends to us when we realize how great our Lord is and how small we are. And with a strong arm God disperses proud people and kicks the mighty ones off thrones. The Most High raises up *humble* people and gives delicious food to the hungry, while the rich, lined up with their hands out, God sends away.

"The Almighty has sent help to Israel, God's servant, remembering the promise of mercy made so long ago to Abraham and his children. A promise for all time!"

The women embraced a third time.

"You have to tell me everything, Mary." Elizabeth pulled back and slipped her arm through Mary's.

"And you as well! Here you are, Cousin, expecting a baby!"

"And at my age! Let me tell you, we had an angel visit—"

"Gabriel?"

"Yes!"

Busy, busy!

"He struck Zechariah speechless!"

"I can certainly understand that."

"Haven't we all wanted to do the same?"

Mary laughed. "When did it happen?"

"At the temple. Gabriel told him I was going to become pregnant, and you know Zechariah. He didn't believe it at first."

Oh, dear.

"But that's just Zechariah! He never believes anything at first."

"Tell that to an archangel!"

Tell an archangel anything. I dare anybody.

"So Gabriel struck him speechless. He still can't talk! The angel said his mouth would remain shut until the baby is born. Who is to be named John, by the way."

"'God is merciful.' The perfect name."

"Isn't it? God has been merciful to me."

"To us all!" cried Mary, fully believing in those mercies amid the saddest set of circumstances I could have imagined for her. My Mary. The Helper of The Most High, the Merciful Creator who carries the morning in arms of light and sets it upon the horizon. I know horizons. I know when light breaks. I've watched it love away the darkness more than any four-footed beast on this sphere ever has. The light always dispels the darkness. It can be no other way.

Mercy to us all indeed, even here now, in Bethlehem. Especially now, for in a moment God always enters the world, the world that was never left behind to begin with.

The night has reached its darkest and soon the sun will rise. Unaware of its own perfection, the red heifer still sleeps by the manger. Perfect red heifers are a rare sacrifice, their ashes mixed with water from a running source, namely the Pool of Siloam and used sparingly. They render a person clean after they have touched a corpse, literally, having felt death.

In many ways, in a land in which being unclean is a sort of death, an acceptable form of banishment, I suppose the heifer brings a human back into life of sorts, into community, into togetherness.

I have heard much talk of the Messiah since he came to us. To be born through Mary. To be born tonight. And perhaps, like the heifer, he will somehow bring the living dead back to life, to be born in all hearts, and perhaps, someday, to be born as all humans, to revive them all again, just as God breathed life into their very first one.

Oh, humans. Oh, humans. My toil is easy compared to yours. I rise, I stand, I bear your burdens, and when you lift them from my back, they are gone. But you; you carry your burdens, shouldering them even when there are none, taking them on when you might choose otherwise.

Perhaps this new baby, our Jesus, will change that.

Mankind will seek Him to take away the burdens so rife: oppression, isolation, thirst, hunger, exposure. And perhaps he will. But I would like to think he will first remove that which causes all of those things, and maybe I am just a stupid old beast who nobody thinks should know better, but I know what that thing is.

What is it, Old Is? You might ask.

The refusal to believe something so very simple. I remember hearing the prophet-king David's words long ago during his reign, "I'm confident that I will see God's goodness in the land of the living."

Confidence. Trust. Knowing God is good.

If humankind really knew this, everything would change once they agreed to live like it. More sharing, more weeping together, more meals, more love, more working together, and nobody would die without a hand to hold.

Someone stirs inside the house as the first light touches the sky, blue and refined, erasing the stars far away. The stable occupants will follow suit as they awaken to the tune of birds and the doves that roost in the rafters. So I will find this moment to echo the poet's words, for truly, *I have seen God's goodness in the land of Israel, and his name is Jesus.*

MARY'S REALIZATION

Humans carry their heaviest
burdens deep within them.
Better a heavy load of bricks
over that any day.

ST.IS

~ 14 ~

Given the circumstances, Mary tried her best. Elizabeth served delicious food, hummed happily and grew in excitement and girth as the babies grew. But Mary's heart grew heavier at the loss of her beloved Joe. Mary took me on walks and poured out her heart. We sat on an outcropping of rock overlooking the rift.

"I know it was the right thing to do, Issy. I was made to say yes to this, but as each day draws on without Joe, and wondering what life will be like for me, for Jesus, without that kind of love I had been looking forward to—" she sighed, "well, I don't know. I had been hoping he would just accept things, take the child as his own, and we could move elsewhere, but then ... Oh!

"Issy! To be the father of the Messiah can only mean one thing for him. As the head of the family, he would have to die before the baby within me could become what he is born to become. The Messiah cannot have an authority over him, can he?

"Issy!"

I had no words.

"I understand. This has been so much more for him! This is a life or death decision, isn't it?"

She sagged, the weight of what her beloved bore in silence bearing down on her.

"I have nowhere, Issy. I cannot ask this of Joe. Elizabeth will soon give birth. I cannot return to my family. I just don't know."

With God as the baby's Father, I had an idea.

"But I do know one thing. I'm not alone."

Of course not. Not with Old Is here.

"I have God's promises. I have my son. And yes—" she scratched my ears, "I always have you, Issy."

She knows me.

Nevertheless, the air felt heavy.

When we returned to the house, three months after our arrival in Hebron, Elizabeth began to labor. Mary helped the rest of the women who attended her. The day remained quiet until the pains picked up a rhythm that gave little time for resting in between. In the night, John arrived, the messenger whose very name proclaimed The Most High is a merciful Creator that never leaves nor forsakes the children of God.

Here in the stable, a fine hand descends upon my neck like one of the doves as she coos in the day. "Rest now, Issy," Mary whispers. "You brought me to this place. You've guarded me. You've been with me every step on this journey. Rest." She leads me to a bed of fresh straw.

She has no idea how many miles I walked to get here.

We've still got miles to go together, but I don't want to tell her that now. The soft bedding cushions my flank and she is right, it's now time for Issy to rest.

"I love you, little friend," she whispers.

I squeak softly and she smiles, her sweetness the last thing I see as my eyes close and sleep settles on me like Mary's tender caress.

ISSY THE TRADER

I've been more places, walked
more miles, seen more things
than you have. And you know
what? I'm still just a donkey.

~ 15 ~

A week after the birth of John, the new baby was in real danger of being named *Zechariah* after his father. Nobody believed Elizabeth or seemed to be moved one iota at her insistence that his name was John. Not should be John. Was John.

We are named, you see, for a reason perhaps beyond what we know. But I know. At least this time around. I am named Issy after the nearby tribe of Issachar who was brilliant enough to choose the donkey as its symbol. And—come closer—the tribespeople of Issachar are known for their intellectual pursuits! They are scholars, philosophers, theologians, surveyors of the known, explorers of the unknown.

Now, the true story of how I came to be called Issy in the house of Mary is this:

Long after bearing the prophet, I was traded in Damascus after years, many years, with a trader possessing an adventurous slant. My name was Delight, and though my time with the family was difficult due to the nature of their work, I finally lived a life of appreciation and good care. I carried many generations to faraway lands and back again to be reunited with their families. I'd rather walk a thousand miles than go into battle even for a day, let it be known.

Amos, my final trader, died without children in a land far to the east. After local officials dealt with his possessions, I was taken to be traded, my heart fainting within me to a degree I had never felt before. This had been my family for longer than any others over all these centuries. Nevertheless, I allowed myself to be led to the trading floor. Me, Delight, the grand donkey trader. Oh, yes! I was engaged in the trade of trading as much as any of the humans.

And I was being traded.

What else could I do?

Oh, the humiliation for one already so low!

My very being cried out to God. "How much longer, oh, Most High, until I see Your Messiah? How much longer shall I wander the earth in wait for the coming of Your Kingdom? Oh, kind Creator, please, may he come soon."

As I stood in the corral, my teeth were harshly examined, my tail lifted, and my ears were jostled and pulled occasionally—as if that said absolutely anything about me. Oh my. My heart began to melt beneath the shadow of despair. Oh, my Lord, I cannot do this, anymore. Please, take me home. Please release me from this arduous vocation. Please release me from heartbreak and sameness. Release me, I pray, Most High, release me from this sad and sorrowful sod.

I wished I had never been—

"*Little Donkey*," I heard The Most High whisper. It was not a tidal wave or a strong and mighty roar like increasing wind picking up the fire in a starry desert camp.

Still. All.

"*Sweet Donkey, once more, dear one. Once more is all I ask. Will you go with Me once more?*"

And I bowed my head further down and received a kiss between my long ears, a kiss of love, the kiss of Light Itself. And I said *yes* to that. Yes, I did. Yes, I yessed.

You bet I did.

At that point, a being so bright I could barely make out the features of a face appeared before me. Oh, the love. The love.

It was the Christos, Lord of All, the Beloved One Who sits at the Right Hand of The Most High. Lord of Angels. Lord of Humanity. Lord of Donkeys. Lover of All—Fully Divine Human in Perfect Expression of the Creator. I saw it all in those eyes. Worlds upon worlds upon worlds, and this world, loved every bit as much by God, ready for the anointing oil of the Christos to sanctify it in and by its all-consuming love, to light it aflame with passions and abilities and chance after chance to love and be loved. I saw it right there.

And love's yesses were destined to outweigh the nos of indifference and hatred. I saw it. And I added mine unto it.

Yes, O, Lord of the Donkeys, too. Yes. I will move forward into the unknown once more. Yes, and yes, and yes again and again. All the yesses I might ever proclaim.

"Sold!" the following moment to a donkey trader bound the next day for the town of Nazareth. Eventually I was purchased by Joachim the older, put into commission as a pack animal, and delivered to Mary, who, year by year grew in love, goodness, and favor with God.

She is most beautiful human being I had ever known. Along with her son, this Messiah, who met me just when I needed him most.

It will be some time before this baby grows old enough to begin anointing the world as the Messiah is called to do as fully loving, fully trusting, fully engaged witness to the current work of The Most High in the world. But the quiet anointing has already begun. The anointing of yet another birth in the town of Bethlehem, but this time a star appears, angels proclaim God's glory, shepherds adore, and a mother cries out in a stable as a garden of animals surround her like living flowers in a field, all present for God's first, newborn kiss.

It will be some time before I carry him into Jerusalem as is my fate, the delivery of a King. And what will they do with this King? Will they crown him truly? Ignore him? Or will they kill him?

Knowing his mother, he may be crowned or killed, but I doubt he will ever be ignored. I have lived a long time, and prophets have been killed for far, far less. So rest Messiah, rest. Old Is knows. Is has chosen your side, for The Most High only arrives in purity and perfection upon the word YES.

Amen. Amen. Amen.

DESERTED!

He wasn't the first man to desert a woman in need, I can tell you that!

ST.IS

~ 16 ~

Not long after John was named, Simon arrived bearing a message from Joe. "I will make you my wife, Mary. An angel told me in a dream to do so. I love you."

"Go, Mary!" said Elizabeth. "You have to! Go tomorrow!" And she kissed her cheeks.

We made for Nazareth the next day. It was a happier trip with Mary and Simon back to their usual cheerful banter. About fifteen miles from Nazareth, however, Mary decided to investigate the truth of Nazareth toward her.

"What has my family been saying, Simon?"

"I was hoping you wouldn't ask that, Mary."

And here I am wondering what took her so long!

"Well?"

Simon dropped his gaze to the ground briefly. "I think you can tell me that."

True.

"But mine would merely be a good guess. Good guesses mean nothing at the time, all guesses are simply that, Simon. There's always a chance you could be, and actually might be, wrong."

Simon stopped us by a stream. "Let's let Issy drink while we talk."

Well, that was okay, I guessed, as long as we maintained the appropriate distance for these ears to hear.

"Look Simon," Mary began. "I have been avoiding this question for months. I'm pregnant. Do they know that?"

"Yes, Joe told them not long after you left."

"Did he say who the baby's father is?"

"Only that it's not his.... Mary—"

"Simon, I'm not asking for anything other than the facts here. I don't need opinion if you're worried you'll have to give yours and hurt my feelings."

"It's a hard thing, Cousin. I hate thinking of you in this manner. That's why. I'm not rejoicing or rubbing my hands or saying you got what you deserved. None of that. I love you."

Mary crumbled to the ground, finally! And she wept there on the banks of the creek. "I'm so scared," she kept saying, over and over again. "I know God is on my side, but I've read the prophets. None of them were immune to the ways the world sees that which is holy."

"I don't know what you mean, Mary."

Mary dried her face with the hem of her head covering and leaned up against me while I continued to drink, and was that water good! "The father of my child is the Holy Spirit."

Time stiffened.

Simon stared at her, mouth hanging open before disbelief tightened his features like wet linen drying in the hot sun. "Wait." He held flattened hands parallel to the ground. "Okay. I think I must have misheard you. Did you say *The Holy Spirit*, as in, 'the Spirit of God came upon him and he prophesied' or 'the Spirit of God came upon him and he slew thousands of people with the jawbone of an ass?'"

Thankfully, not mine.

"Is that the kind of Spirit you mean is the actual father of your child?"

Mary nodded. "I know it sounds crazy, but—"

"It sounds more than crazy, Mary. It's blasphemous even to a skeptic like me! Who in the world do you think you *are* to claim such a thing? You're *pregnant*! Before the actual marriage! And you have found a way to directly blame this on the Almighty?"

"I just—"

"What happened that you should even think such a thing?"

"An angel appeared and told me I would become pregnant—"

"An angel? I know I'm not the smartest man in Nazareth, but I didn't think you thought I was stupid, Mary. An angel?"

"But he spoke, Simon. I heard him."

Simon paused, then, "No! I don't care what you heard. People hear things all the time."

"Issy was with me. You could tell she was looking at something too!"

"I'm supposed to take a donkey's word for it now?"

Yes! Not that I'll waste a single word on you, Simon.

"You know, Mary, I have always been here for you. Mary and Simon, cousins and friends. You're the peculiar one of the family and even my own parents have wondered about my devotion to you, but I've always known you were special. Do you agree with that?"

"Yes, Simon. You have. I've always felt safe with you."

Until now.

I stopped drinking and stared at Simon.

"You and Issy go away together into the countryside. You leave the house at night. You do almost whatever you want—"

"That's not true, Simon! You know what life is like in Nazareth, and for a girl?"

"Don't, Mary. You know what I mean. You take liberties and hope nobody minds, hope nobody says anything, and if they do, you come out with all the right words. And yes, they are true, but they aren't always kind, Mary. Be that as it may, all right. But you can't expect words like the ones you just said to be considered even for a second by anyone."

"But Elizabeth—"

"Elizabeth? You want to use her to justify your own state? Mary, you're crazy! Maybe Elizabeth was just playing along to keep you safe! Did you ever consider that?"

"No, I—"

"You will probably be stoned for this and I want nothing to do with it. I'm sorry. I have to go."

He turned and started up the road, wiping his eyes with the back of his hand.

"Without me?" Mary cried. "Simon!"

He held up a hand and continued forward.

"What are you going to tell people?"

He spoke nothing.

"I trusted you!" Mary yelled.

But Simon kept walking.

Just me and Mary now; I would get her home. I would.

Mary wept, whispering as the night grew dark and a covering of clouds hid the stars. We hid in the bushes until morning light. "I am not alone. I am not alone. I am not alone."

No, you're definitely not, my sweet lady. Not as long as I am breathing.

MARY AND JOE

I walked the earth. I witnessed the splendors of Egypt and Mesopotamia. I watch the riches of men flow back and forth between them like the tide. And all I know is that true love, food, water, and a sturdy roof to keep my ears dry is about the best ending of the day imaginable. Oh, and don't forget a good roll in the hay.

ST.IS

~ 17 ~

Joe met us at the entrance to Nazareth the next day, rushing toward us as Mary pulled me up to a stop.

"Simon came to Sepphoris to tell me what happened a little while ago. I set out right away," he said. "Are you all right, Mary? If I had known I would have come to you much earlier than this."

"Oh, Joe!" She slipped from my back and into his arms. The scandal had already taken over like weeds, choking out anything even close to the truth, so why not give them more to talk about? "Has he said anything about the angel?"

He pulled back, hands still circling her upper arms. "Did you tell him that?"

"I did." She hugged her body. "I can't believe I was that stupid."

"It's okay, Mary. We all say things we regret later. He didn't seem to be overcome with anger or disappointment. In fact, he said he's going to go to Capernaum to an uncle's house for a while."

"Uncle David." Mary's body sagged. "I hope that's good for us."

"It is. Simon left this morning. He told me he wouldn't bring your state of mind out in the open. Now I know what he meant. He says he will leave you in my hands."

I felt it, I did. I felt her sorrow flow into me at losing her favorite relative, the one who was more like a brother than Joachim or Eli would ever be. "It's going to be like this, then? For the rest of our lives?"

"No. It isn't. At least I hope not! My advice is that we keep that evening to ourselves, Mary. And don't forget, God told me not to be afraid to take you as my wife. That sounds like a promise to me. And I hope it sounds like one to you, too."

She nodded. "Two angels can't be wrong."

Three. I remembered that day at the auction. Although that was more than an angel.

"Let's get you home."

Amid stares and jeers from the villagers and family members, Joe led us. The young man, having been faced with a difficult decision had made the most righteous choice available to him. He kept his head high, his gaze open and yielding, peace surrounding him and his beloved and her donkey.

You see, nobody he saw or heard on that slow walk down the crooked lanes could break through the utter joy ringing in his heart at being united with his Mary, his dear Mary, his beloved partner. The love that flowed from him warmed my tired body and filled my heart with hope's blessed note.

He led us into the small stable attached to the left side of his home, fresh straw already spread, fresh hay in the manger, and water in the trough. A donkey's paradise.

They made their promises to one another beneath a canopy of Mary's cloth and God's blessing.

ELI AND JOACHIM

If you can't at the very least be happy for others, God help you, because you're going to need it.

ST.IS

~ 18 ~

The months passed and Mary's growing belly filled up the outer reaches of her gown. She sang to the babe inside of her, spun fleece brought to her by Joe, and made yarn and woolen garments Joe took to the market in Sepphoris. She received no one.

Mary hadn't returned to her father's house for good reason. One night in the stable soon after we arrived from Elizabeth's, the door slammed open, banging against the wall.

"Hey, what are you doing?" Joe called, reaching the door before both brothers had entered. He barred Eli from making it across the threshold, but Joachim rushed Mary, who backed up toward the stable opening.

"Look, you harlot. The shame you have brought to our family—" he grated through his rage, "is worth killing you for. You know that, don't you?"

Joe left Eli and hurried to Mary's side. "Joachim, stop this. You've entered my home without my agreement to it. I suggest you leave right now."

"Suggest?" His tunic bloated with disdain. "Figures."

Joe stood in front of Mary. "It's time for you both to leave." Shifting, he put his arm around her shoulder. "Are you all right, dearest?"

Mary nodded as I stepped into the gated opening of the shared wall between stable and house.

If you boys want a fight, well ... Joe might be a holy man, but Old Is isn't.

And don't forget, I can fight with both front feet and back feet.

Mary's hand settled on my head.

"Eli?" Joe asked. "What did you come here to *actually* say?"

Joachim reddened, pulled back his fist and hesitated enough for Joe to see where it was going. When the fist shot forward Joe caught it in his hand, his strong, stone worker's hand.

Squeeze, Joe, squeeze!

But he just threw it back toward its owner.

Joachim hit himself in the face.

I brayed and brayed and brayed.

They moved toward the door to get away from the sound.

Joe remained calm. "Eli?"

"Just this. If she walks over our threshold, we'll drag her out to the stoning pit." He turned to Mary. "Our mother has been crying night and day over your failure to let her give her daughter the wedding she deserves. Our father sits in the corner night after night in shame. And we are laughed at. We don't want you dead, sister, but you must know, we cannot look the other way."

"And we wouldn't want to!" cried Joachim.

"Speak for yourself, brother," said Eli. "I didn't mean for things to play out like this, Joe. I meant for this to be peaceably done."

Joachim reddened more.

Eli grabbed his younger sibling by the sleeve. "Let's go. I will speak to father about your behavior. There are ways to do this, you know, Joachim. We don't need any more gossip and we have more shame right now than we can bear."

Eli pulled Joachim out of the house. Neither looked back.

Mary hurried to the door and watched them walk down the lane. Several people had gathered in their own doorways to listen in on the family happenings. She threaded her arm through Joe's as he closed us back in and leaned into him, her head resting upon him in utter trust.

"I'm sorry," she whispered. "I'm nothing but trouble to you."

"You're worth every bit of it, Mary."

"My family, too?"

"Yes." He squeezed her to his side. "Although they take more work."

They smiled into each other's faces, not smiles of joy, but smiles in sorrow; soft smiles with sad eyes that say together we will weather this day, and tomorrow, and whatever comes after that.

This is love. This is goodness. And this gives me hope.

I laid down in my soft bed of fresh straw.

You see, all I ever wanted for Mary was for her to spend her life with a man who realized how precious she truly is. And she found him.

GLORY AND BLESSING

Mary's songs sounded
perfect to me.

ST.IS

~ 19 ~

Of course, Mary couldn't see the heavenly host surrounding her during this time in Nazareth like I could. But God doesn't abandon the created ones whether they are walking on two feet or being carried within their mother. This new family was no exception.

Though she couldn't see the celestial singers they somehow joined in praise together.

Glory, glory, glory to the Lord, the Almighty God
Creator of the spheres
Lover of humankind
Beautiful, gracious, and full of lovingkindness.
Holy is Your name. Holy is Your name.
You have joined us in our abandonment.
You have remembered us in our desolation.
You have raised us in our humiliation.
You have accepted us in our rejection.
You are our hope in our despair.
Our light in the darkness.
Our joyful song.
Surrendered in Your favor we sing:
Glory, glory, glory to the Lord of Hosts.
The beginning, the end,
From everlasting to everlasting.
You are God.

Mary and I sat as close as we could throughout the day, the woman of the house, and the jenny of the stable. She sang and spun while I rested more than I had in many years. One evening, while Mary sang, weaving near the entry to the stable, surrounded by hope and favor as she worked, Joe arrived home with a bundle of dried figs.

"I found this on the road, my love. It's normally a busy stretch of road, none but me walked down it right then. And there it was."

"A treat from heaven, it seems. Or a very careless person."

One and the same. One and the same.

Joe twisted off a fig from its stem and held it out to his wife. "Mary, look. God has shown us our path is filled with the sweetness of the Lord's plan for us. We need not fear to follow where the Spirit leads for the sake of this child. Even as the fig leaf once covered our shame, the plant has blossomed, given fruit, and is now ready to be consumed in agreement that we will see the goodness of the Lord in the land of the living. And his name will be called Jesus."

And so Joe prophesied, and so has it ever been true.

They shared the fig as the angels lifted up their hearts in praise and when we all came back down to earth what was left of us was bound together in trust.

We would all be taken care of because God was here.

And when God is here, there's no need to ever feel afraid.

JOACHIM'S REVENGE

I have lived many centuries so this I
know for sure, nothing is impossible
with God. But I have a secret to tell.
This life you are living today holds all
the time you need to realize this for
yourself.

ST.IS

~ 20 ~

During the harvest one night, someone knocked on the door.

Joe and Mary slept.

The knock sounded again and Joe rose, wary. "Issy," he whispered.

Standing up, I squeaked softly and he opened the gate. "Just in case."

I am always ready *just in case.* Donkeys are made for *just in case.* Donkeys adore *just in case.*

He cracked open the door to reveal a thin strip of night sky blocked by shadow. "Who is it?"

"It's Eli," a voice whispered. "I don't come in harm. But I would like this to be as secret as possible."

Joe stepped back and pulled the door in halfway, shutting it quickly and quietly behind Mary's oldest brother.

Mary awakened and raised her head. "Eli?" She leaned up on one elbow. "Did you get a new robe?"

That's your question? Oh, my goodness, dear mistress!

"Yes, Mary." He knelt down where she lay.

"Is everything all right at home?"

"Yes. Except for Joachim. Joe?" He motioned to his brother-in-law. "You should come over here." He took his sister's hand.

When Joe knelt, Eli whispered. "Joachim cannot bear the shame our family has been forced to shoulder. It has begun to throw him over the edge into that madness that only allows for revenge."

"What should we do?" Mary turned to Joe.

Eli rested his hand on his sister's shoulder and looked over at Joe. "You have to head to Bethlehem for the census, yes?"

"I do. We're leaving in a week's time."

"That's what Joachim thought. She can't stay here alone." He turned to Mary. "You can't stay here alone. And I can't be here to protect you or I will be seen as guilty." Back to Joe. "Can you take her with you to Bethlehem?"

Mary, almost fully pregnant, was ready to deliver in weeks or perhaps days if the times delivered that to us. Her eyes rounded. "Oh, but all that way at my stage? I can hardly imagine."

"I know, sister. But the alternative is unthinkable. Please, this is the best answer to all of this."

"What will happen while I am gone?" Joe asked. "This house? Our animals?"

"I have an answer in the stable yard. Is it alright if I ask him in?"

"I have no idea who you're talking about," Joe said, "but yes, of course."

Eli arose, walked through the gate, past me and into the yard. He returned twofold, the second person rushing to fall at the feet of his cousin. "Mary," Simon whispered a hoarse cry of the heart. "Forgive me, cousin. You have never been unfaithful to me. I believe you."

"So do I," said Eli. "Simon told me everything when I was in Capernaum a few weeks ago and I prayed to the Lord for an answer to my question of whether or not this could be so, and I was answered to my satisfaction."

Another angel? Eli would definitely assume everybody would think he was crazy. Even I knew that.

The explanation surprised nobody, however. It was all Eli was offering. Mary knew just like I did it was all there would ever be.

"Thank you, Eli," she said in the darkness. "Thank you, Simon. I have missed you both so much."

"Mary." Eli took her hand. "I cannot stand beside you. Had I the resources to do so, I would take you away from this myself if I could." He turned once more to Joe and placed her hand in his. "Joe, as her older brother, I am placing my trust in you to do what I cannot, what I wish I could do if I had the faith you do." He released Mary's hand and Joe held tight.

"I will pledge that the faith that I have will always be for her good, Eli."

I felt Mary's heart split open with joy. "Thank you, brother."

They rejoiced. What else was there for it? The lost had been found, all that had wandered away from love came back to serve it, and what was needed for our family to live together in grace was provided even in the hearts of those who loved Mary most.

The journey ahead wouldn't be easy. Especially for my mistress. But love was already on the job taking care of things right here in Nazareth.

"Perhaps someday," Eli said as he rose to go, "God will make a way for us all to be reunited."

"Here in Nazareth?" Mary raised her eyebrows.

Eli reached out and squeezed her shoulder. "God parted the seas, yes?"

Oh, yes, the Almighty parts seas!

The Lord of Hosts rules the seas and holds tight the sun in the sky. God clears trails in the wilderness and lights the darkness with shining pools of hope, carrying us on the wind of the Spirit's love.

I have lived many centuries so this I know for sure: nothing is impossible with God. But I have a secret to tell. This life you are living today holds all the time you need to realize this for yourself.

BETHLEHEM, BETHLEHEM

Humans like to say there are only two
certainties in life, death and taxes. But
they seem much more concerned
about taxes than death. I still haven't
figured that one out.

ST.IS

~ 21 ~

We left in the dark hours of morning for Bethlehem. Rome decided in typical Roman fashion that "all the world should be taxed."

All the world.

Truly, they meant all the empire should be taxed. But like all empires, Rome misconstrued that the future held their way of doing things as a matter of common sense to everybody everywhere.

Many of those human beings in togas haven't seen the lands I've seen. Even the people clad in metal and the cured skins of animals haven't gone to the edges of the earth as this little donkey has, where people live as they have decided with no thought to Rome whatsoever.

And many thrive.

However, that didn't matter to Mary and Joe. Joe had to register so he could be taxed according to his birthplace and according to how many people lived in his household. And animals, too. Emperor Augustus had changed everything along the lines of taxes. It was better than before but—

Oh, taxes, taxes! The hours I have been forced to listen to human beings complaining about taxes!

Nevertheless, the road welcomed us again, that same road leading from Nazareth to Jerusalem. The same twists and turns, the same potential for thieves and hijackers, pickpockets, and ruffians looking for conflict.

"Are you sure there's room at your father's house?" Mary asked the night before we were to arrive in Bethlehem.

"Well, I don't know for sure in the sense of a promise, Mary, but I am as confident as I can be with having sent a message you're coming along."

We slept close, the smell of harvested barley meeting us like a cherished old friend that never fails to visit once a year. Mary walked much of the journey the next day, unable to comfortably support her spine on my back with the load she carried in her belly. Poor Mary and human child-bearers in general. Their babies rest upon their hips and other organs, smashing their insides in very strange directions. I don't know how they do this thing. We animals have it so much better.

Don't tell the humans that, though. They wouldn't believe it anyway.

Bethlehem appeared as darkness fell, a collection of stars in the folds of the night sky lifting to reveal sunset's deep prism beneath it. The road dipped toward the city gate, people still streaming in from outside their natal providence to be counted by Rome and to declare their wealth. Before now, taxation was done by tax farmers, or publicans, the shadiest bunch of … Well, let us simply say they were experts at extracting money from the living and the dead.

We threaded through the gate in a rope of humanity, knots of people at the entrance, pulled through by the need for a little water, a little food, and a good night's rest. The main street funneled us through the marketplace and past the ancient wells, as Joe led us to the house of Jacob, his father, in the City of David, in the land of Judah.

Now Judah, to refresh the memory, was the brother of the famous Joseph who saved the people of Israel from a famine. Judah was the brother who sold his brother Joseph. Sold his very brother into slavery! Does it get harder-hearted? And here we were, entering into the territory belonging to Judah's descendants for God to bring forth the Messiah.

Don't tell me The Most High has little appreciation for irony. The Lord specializes in it, but in the case of God, it's called redemption. The kind of redemption so perfect for the transgression it can only be the outworking of a Creator who perfectly ties things together—not by changing them into something unrecognizable, but singing them into a love song that never ends, a song that brings the most discordant-seeming melodies together into one harmonious tone.

Here, O Israel, the Lord our God, the Lord is One.

And here we were, bringing together all that once was a mystery into all that can come to be here: the realm of the Christos in this place and time. He is here already really, safe in the pregnant belly of a young woman from Nazareth, scorned by her parents, wanted by her vengeful brother, but held in the arms of Love. Not just the love of The Most High, but the love of Joe and a donkey she calls her friend.

Just down the lane from the house of Joe's father, Mary slipped down from my back and exclaimed, "Oh, dear!" as she landed.

Heads turned, but Joe dipped his by hers. "Are you all right?"

"My waters. They have released."

A stream flowed from under the hem of her gown over the dusty earth, beneath my legs, and into the roots of nearby fig tree. "We're almost there, dearest," Joe said, putting his arm around her waist and drawing her body into his. "Lean on me. It won't be much longer."

Humans can be so wrong and not even know it.

Joseph led us into the family stable five minutes later. He spread a fresh bed of straw for the both of us. "Wait here with Issy, Mary."

"Joe!" somebody yelled. "You're here!"

My ears are so valuable to me at times like this. Too bad they're not to anybody else.

"Father! I have Mary with me," he said, as he let himself through the stable gate and into the house.

The evening was bubbling like a good lentil stew, lamps glowing and people

123

catching up. The women were bringing food in from the communal kitchen down the street, and people sat at every available surface after their long journeys. And the aroma? My goodness!

"The guest room is already taken, son," said Jacob, a small man in brown robes, a giant gray beard concealing his chest and stomach. "Your message came too late. You're going to have to stay in the stable. My apologies."

"She's in labor, Father."

Silence.

"Ruth!" his father cried out to Joseph's mother. "We need the stable cleared of everybody. Let them sleep on the floor in here. Mary's going to give birth to our grandchild."

"Father, we—"

"Send Ezekiel out to fetch the midwife!" a woman cried, and a general upheaval began, the same upheaval that always begins when a human gets ready to enter the world.

I stood back up as Joseph's mother and several women rushed in ready to assess the situation at hand and made my way to guard the stable door. Donkeys have their young in stables all the time, but humans? Well, I'm sure it's happened before, but I had yet to see it.

Ruth leaned down and laid a hand on Mary's head. "The midwife is coming, but in the meantime, we will get you comfortable."

"Ma'am, I need—"

"Shh, dear. A baby is coming. All is well."

"But—"

"There's always time for talk, daughter. But now is the time for action and I will tell you this. I believe God brought you and this child to us, just like he gave us Joe."

"Thank you," Mary whispered.

"The Lord's mercies are new every morning, child."

I watched people milling down the lane, those gathering for the census and the festival which was set to begin the next day. The *Feast of Tabernacles*, as the humans call it, which involves setting up temporary structures and celebrating the harvest, had brought many to the vicinity of Jerusalem. If everything went smoothly, the family would introduce its newest member the very first day of Sukkot, the first of two all-out festival days.

Donkeys love festival days. A day off for most of the family beasts, a little more food, rest, and plenty of rolling around, is one of the practical reasons I like sojourning in Israel.

The harvest is in, everybody. The Bread of the living is coming. The Wine of God's love is getting ready to flow over all this land. The Shelter of The Most High, the Abiding Place of the Almighty One, is here. The ever-present Tabernacle come to welcome wandering hearts as creation opens up this very night to welcome its Creator face to face.

The night lengthened as the time between Mary's labor pains shortened. The men were all gone. Women and beasts, you see, the lowly ones, well, we welcomed the King of Kings, and do you know why? We are downcast enough to recognize the pure bravery a human exhibits at merely being born into this beautiful yet tense, glorious yet weighted world.

Oh, Jesus. Oh, Jesus. Come, come.

Come quickly.

Come for good.

While donkeys have more than one trick, we only have one track, and mine is to bear the Messiah.

ST.IS

~ 22 ~

I wonder how many will take this night and make of it what they will? How many will imagine Mary bearing the perfect one perfectly, no pain or inconvenience?

So, I will tell you this. Birth is not easy.

This doesn't make it wrong.

We donkeys know a little bit about discomfort. We accept it as of our lives so we also know to enjoy the water when we get it, the feed when it comes our way, and the fresh air at all times.

But I've noticed humans are different. They're not very good at being humans. There's always something wrong, something to grieve over, and someone to treat like they're not also a human. I'm hoping our Jesus will change that. It's a very tough assignment and I wouldn't want to be in his place.

Surrounded by womanly care, Mary cried out like every other woman I had ever heard giving birth. Her brow was wiped. One of the women gently combed her fingers through Mary's increasingly wet hair and said soft words of encouragement.

A child was coming! And in Israel, every child is God's child.

Most High, may this child show what a kind and loving parent You truly are, forever forgiving and Love everlasting. May they see the kindness and goodness and courage of Your Son so that they may see kindness and goodness and courage in one another as long as time carries them in its arms.

Perhaps this birth, this coming of God's love for humans, will spark in them love for all that God has made, not only for each other, but for donkeys like Old Is. Oh, for all the donkeys, and the cows, and the sparrows, too.

Even the lilies, so beautiful, so accepting of rain and sun and holy goodness. All of us. All of us. All of us.

I'm a hopeful creature to be certain, and oh, joy of all joys!

"He is here!" his grandmother cried.

Every one moved in to see as Ruth held him close and patted his behind. "Come, come. Tell us you've arrived."

Nobody breathed.

No sound escaped from the little one. They flicked his feet, jostled his body, and though only ten seconds had passed, a flurry began with a series of gasps.

But my Mary reached out her arms, folded her baby inside, shook him lightly and said, "Little one! Little one! Wake up! It's time to begin."

Several women looked at each other and shrugged, but Mary peered into the glittering eyes of her Son. She kissed his head, and, I would like to tell you he smiled like the Divine. But instead, he yelled.

Oh, and yelled.

And ten minutes later, he was still yelling.

"I think he likes the sound of his voice!" one of the women joked.

Now, that I understood.

"He will be good at singing!" another laughed.

If this child didn't like the sound of his voice, nobody else would. And I have a strong donkey feeling, that the note he sings will be of love, not hate; peace, not war; health not division.

May the song of Jesus be brayed in utter abandon from this night forward. May the song of donkeys echo the note of God. And may humans realize it is the song they, too, have always been meant to sing.

GET READY JOE

So you were looking for an ending? Oh, my friend. The Story has just begun.

ST.IS

~ 23 ~

Joe loads some water jars on my back. "Come on, Issy. Let's get to the well. A lot of people are coming today. I don't know how we're going to eat all that food, and if Father asks me to dance ... Lord, have mercy." He laughed.

I squeaked. He rubbed my nose.

Humans and their celebrations.

I hope they never stop.

To be continued...

Thank You For Reading

To learn more about The Salish Sea Press and St.Is,
visit us at https://salishsea.press/

Follow The Salish Sea press on social media.
Facebook and Instagram: thesalishseapress

And don't forget about Old Is!
Facebook and Instagram: asassysidekick

Other Titles by Lisa and Len

Author of 40 books, Lisa's reader favorites are:

Quaker Summer

The Passion of Mary-Margaret

Embrace Me

Author of over 60 books, Len's latest are:

Contextual Intelligence, with Michael Beck

Rings of Fire: Walking in Faith Through a Volcanic Future

Mother Tongue

The Bad Habits of Jesus